Out and About

First published in Great Britain in 1982 by
The Bodley Head Children's Books

This edition published in Great Britain and in the USA in 2008 by
Frances Lincoln Children's Books, 4 Torriano Mews,
Torriano Avenue, London NW5 2RZ
www.franceslincoln.com

British Library Cataloguing
in Publication Data
available on request

ISBN 978-1-84507-725-9

Printed in Singapore

9 8 7 6 5 4 3 2 1

GOING SHOPPING

Sarah Garland

F
FRANCES LINCOLN
CHILDREN'S BOOKS

In you go.

Jump in, dog!

ARP 341

Down the road

and off to the shop.

Out of the car

ARP 341

and into the shop.

Shopping, shopping,

more and more shopping.

Baby!

Pack it all up

and back to the car.

In you go

and home again.